Penguins

Written by
Helen Orme

When you think about the word 'penguin', what picture comes into your mind? Could it be one like this?

These are Emperor penguins. They are big birds; each is about a metre high and weighs about 40 kilogrammes. These penguins live all year round in Antarctica, the large area of land at the South Pole.

Emperor penguins don't mind getting cold. In Antarctica the temperature can be as low as minus 60 degrees centigrade. This is much too cold for humans to survive for very long.

Not all penguins are like Emperor penguins. There are seventeen different sorts of penguins, and they don't all live in Antarctica.

Here are some of them.

King penguin

Rockhopper penguin

Fairy penguin

African penguin

Where do penguins live?

All penguins live south of the Earth's equator, in the southern hemisphere. This is why penguins and polar bears never meet each other! Polar bears only live in the northern hemisphere, near the North Pole.

Many different kinds of penguins do live in Antarctica, or on the islands nearby. These birds are specially adapted to live in very cold places.

But not all penguins live in, or near, Antarctica. This is a Galapagos penguin. These penguins are found only on the Galapagos Islands – which are on the equator.

Galapagos Islands

We saw a picture of an African penguin on page three. These penguins live on the coast of South Africa. They have been hunted for many years, but the good news is that they are now protected.

This is a yellow-eyed penguin. You can probably work out how these animals got their name!

The yellow-eyed penguin is found in New Zealand – and it is the world's rarest penguin. There are only about 4,000 of these penguins left in the world.

Keeping warm

Emperor penguins live in the coldest place on Earth. So how do they keep warm?

Their bodies are specially adapted. Under their skin they have a layer of fat, called blubber, and two layers of feathers.

The feathers nearest to the skin are soft and fluffy, and these hold in the warmth.

Their outer feathers make a tight seal, so the cold winds can't get through. The penguins seal these feathers using oil they produce from a special gland.

Antarctic penguins have another trick. They huddle together to keep warm, and change places often, so that the penguins on the outside get a turn in the middle!

How do Galapagos penguins keep cool?

In the Galapagos Islands it can be very hot, so the Galapagos penguins have a different problem.

A Galapagos penguin enjoying the sunshine.

These penguins have learnt to spread out their wings and fluff out their feathers, to let the air reach their bodies and help keep them cool.

How do penguins move?

Penguins aren't very good at moving on land, but they are very good at moving in the water.

Their wings have become flippers, and their bodies have the right shape for moving through the water at speeds of up to seventeen miles an hour. This is four times faster than the fastest human can swim.

Penguins need to move fast to catch their prey and to avoid being caught by predators.

Penguins can't fly, but they can leap out of the water to take a breath or reach the land.

When penguins walk on land they are very slow – they walk at a speed of less than three miles an hour – but they have learnt to turn themselves into sledges and slide across the ice!

Hunting and eating

Fish is the most important food for penguins. The penguins' beaks have hooks that are specially designed to catch their prey.

Penguins also have backward-facing hairs on their tongues to stop the prey getting away once they have been caught.

Penguins will also eat other sea creatures, such as squid and tiny animals called krill.

Squid

Krill

How do penguins feed their young?

When penguins catch their food, they swallow it and start to digest it. When the penguins get back to their family, they can cough the food up again from their stomach and feed their chicks with it. They use their beaks as spoons to get the food into the mouths of the young penguins.

Some types of penguin parents can digest the food completely and hold it in their stomachs for several days. Then they feed the digested food to the chicks. This is sometimes called penguin milk.

Penguin families

Penguins mate and look after their young in special areas called rookeries.

Looking after a penguin egg is a long, boring job. An Emperor penguin egg can take two months to hatch, and it is the male penguin's job to look after it. For all that time he doesn't eat anything.

Once the chick is hatched, the parents take it in turns to go hunting for food for the chicks.

In icy places, there is nothing that the penguins can use to build nests.

So the egg rests on the penguin's feet and is sheltered by a special warm 'pouch' on the penguin's body.

Some types of penguins build nests out of stones. Sometimes, fights break out as penguin parents try to grab the best stones!

Penguins in danger

Penguins are hunted by other animals for food.

When the penguins are on land, the main danger to them comes from the air. Birds, such as the giant petrel, are always on the look-out for penguin chicks, and weak and sick penguins.

Look out! A leopard seal is on his way!

At sea, creatures such as leopard seals will prey on penguins, especially in winter when food is short.

These predators are all part of the natural world. Many more serious problems for penguins are a result of changes caused by people.

In the past, penguins were hunted by humans because their bodies contained useful oil. Now all penguins are protected from hunting, but there are still problems. Their habitat can be damaged by oil spills and other pollution.

Climate change is another problem. As the sea gets warmer, it has serious effects on the penguins' food supply.

How did penguins get their name?

One idea is that the name comes from the Welsh language. Pen gwyn ('pen gwinn') in Welsh means 'white head'.

But there is a problem. Most penguins have black heads!

Another idea is that the name comes from Latin. In Latin, pinguis means fat. Dutch people called penguins 'fat geese'.

Are penguins fat? You decide!